For Wendy Cooling, Polar Explorer.
Warm wishes — T.M.

For Bump,

with love — G.P-R

ORCHARD BOOKS

338 Euston Road, London NW1 3BH

Orchard Books Australia

Level 17/207 Kent Street, Sydney, NSW 2000

ISBN 978 1 84616 338 8

First published in 2007 by Orchard Books

Text © Tony Mitton 2007

Illustrations © Guy Parker-Rees 2007

1 3 5 7 9 10 8 6 4 2

Printed in China

Orchard Books is a division of Hachette Children's Books,
an Hachette Livre UK company.

Perky Little Penguins

Tony Mitton   Guy Parker-Rees

ORCHARD BOOKS

Perky little penguins

coming out to play,

looking for their playmates...

here they are — hooray!

Lots of little penguins

skimming through the snow,

slipping on the slidy ice,

squeaking as they go.

Perky little penguins
in the wintry weather —

that's how penguins like to play,
waddling round together.

Perky little penguins make a shiny slide. "Wheeeee!" pipe the penguins. "What a whizzy ride!"

Perky little penguins,
as they jump about,
make a squeaky, shrieky noise –
what a squabbly **shout!**

Perky little penguins
are hungry for their lunch,

so off they go to look for it,

in a busy bunch.

Perky little penguins
in the wintry weather —
that's how penguins look for lunch,
leaping out together.

Eager little penguins
jumping in the sea,
"Yay!" shriek the penguins.
"That's the place to be!"

They swirl about,

they whirl about,

splashy, sploshy, splish.

They curl about,

they twirl about,

catching tasty fish.

Perky little penguins in the wintry weather –
that's how penguins like to lunch,
whirling round together.

But what's this on the ice floe?
A little ball of fur?
A sobbing baby seal pup!
Whatever's wrong with her?

"Tell us, baby seal pup,
have you come far?
You're looking rather frightened.
Have you lost your ma?"

"She saw some fish go swimming by and dived into the sea.
The ice floe we were resting on went drifting off with me!"

"Don't worry, baby seal pup, we're sure she's on her way.

But why not, while you're waiting, watch us as we play?"

All the little penguins

try to cheer her up.

And soon she seems
much happier,
a playful little pup!

The penguins do a dippy dance
with silly jigs and wriggles.

And soon the little seal pup
is full of grins and giggles.

Perky little penguins
in the wintry weather –
that's how penguins like to play,
messing round together.

But what's that in the water?
Help, it's coming near!
It's speedy and it's shadowy.
It fills them all with fear.

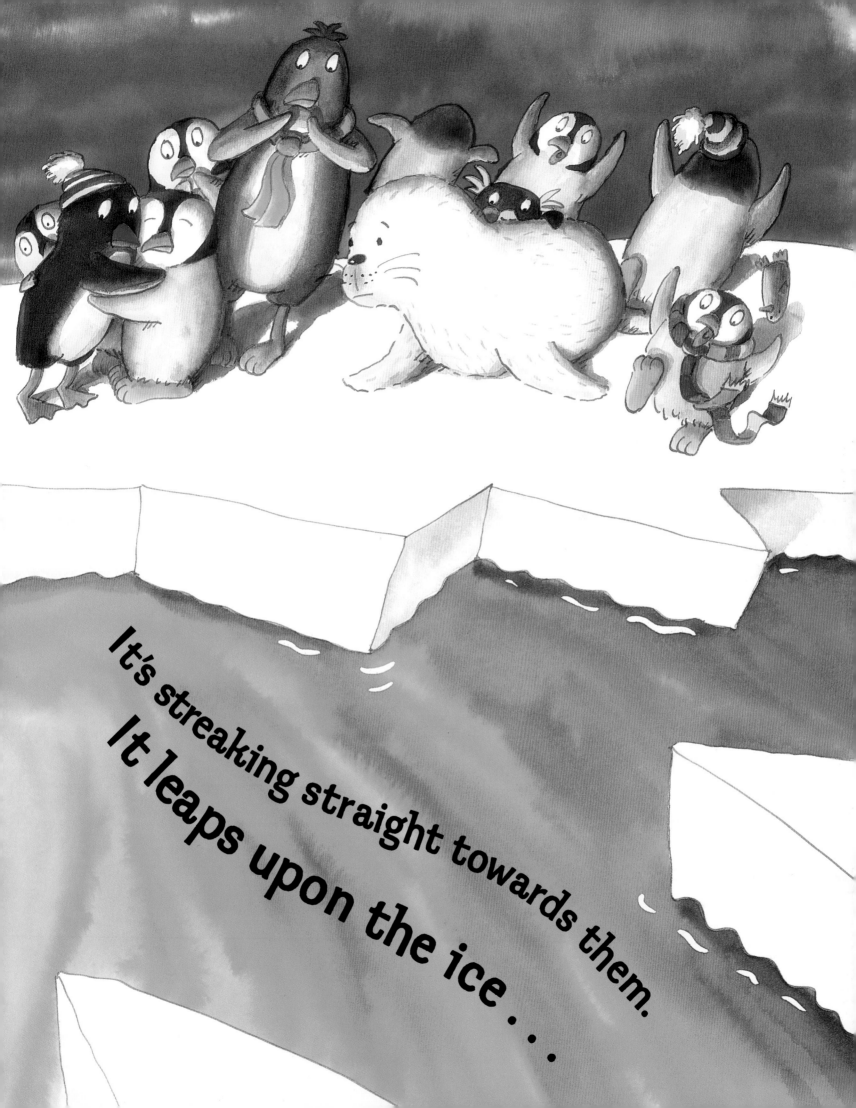

It's streaking straight towards them.
It leaps upon the ice . . .

Seal Pup calls to Mama
with a squeaky little yelp.

Then Mama thanks the penguins
for their kindness and their help.

Mama Seal takes Seal Pup.

They slowly swim away.

Then the penguins realise
it's time to end their day.

Perky little penguins,
how sleepily they go –
waddling and **yawning**,
through the ice and snow.

Home they go together,
back to Mum and Dad.
They tell them all the things they've done
and all the fun they've had.

Sleepy little penguins
in a happy huddle —
that's how penguins like to rest.

What a cosy cuddle!